SEEK TO PLEASE BOOK 1

SEEKING IN ROMANCE

KEKE RENÉE

304 PUBLISHING COMPANY

I want to thank my readers for supporting my characters and being open to all the crazy adventures.

DISCLAIMER

This work of fiction contains strong language and explicit sexual content and is only intended for mature readers. This story may contain unconventional situations, language, and sexual encounters that may offend some readers.This book is for mature readers (18+).

INTRODUCTION

This is a continuation of the *Wet Heat Series* called "Seeking in Romance." This new series deals with different couples. I won't give too much away, but you'll have to follow and subscribe to my newsletter for sneak peeks, updates, and cover reveals for more details.

SYNOPSIS

Maya

I've worked hard to earn my senatorial position. I'm determined to do what's right, and I keep my life free from scandal, but that proves difficult when one night out at Club Seek threatens my career and reputation.

Mason

I've accomplished a lot not using my family's last name. I'm a business owner, and the son of the most powerful man in the state of Tennessee. I find myself on opposite ends of drama when photos leak out about my club after spending time with a sexy woman who's powerful in her own right. Some fun play and a few pictures later, life becomes complicated.

When those scandalous photos are leaked, Maya's life is turned upside down. With everything on the line, including our growing feelings for each other, I wonder if we can rein in the chaos and avoid political suicide for her career?

Every Time We Touch (Wet Heat Series)

"I CAN'T WAIT TO SEE you in what I bought you tonight," Mason groaned over the phone, causing a shiver to run down my spine. I'd received a package at my door, hand delivered and wrapped. I wasn't expecting anything at all. With our lives being as busy as they were, we'd made a deal to not keep in touch. The rules were simple. We met up, we fucked, and then we went our separate ways.

"Mason," I sighed. The sound of his voice alone caused my clit to throb. I ran a hand between my thighs, imagining it was his lips. I ran a hand over the red lace corset, thong, and red five-inch heels laid on top of a black box. A black engraved invitation next to the pile requested my presence tonight.

"Am I hearing distress in your voice, Miss Hill?"

"No, you're hearing the sound of a woman who hasn't had pleasure in a while because of work. It seems your voice is doing something to me, and now I'm running a hand over my breast as I talk with you on the phone."

"You know I don't like it when you touch yourself."

"I guess you'll have to remind me tonight as I wear my new lingerie for you."

"Mhmm. Maya, you know the last thing you want to do is defy me," Mason growled through the phone.

I hung up the phone, leaving him anticipating what our night would be like after the last time we met up. We had tried anal play and brought in new partners.

He made the standard arrangements for me to be picked up and escorted through the back alley of the club, so no one would notice me. The dark-tinted windows of the vehicle were always a must have whenever we planned to meet up. As the newly elected senator in Tennessee Congress, it would be all over the media about a state senator seeking pleasure from a sex club. I would never apologize for my lifestyle, since I was a single woman. But I knew it would hinder me from getting things done correctly for the people who voted me into office. It didn't make the situation any better that the son of the speaker of the house in Congress was the one who owned the club.

CHAPTER 1

SENATOR HILL

"Xavier, calm down; he was helping me before I tripped," Chelsey said, caressing his arm. That seemed to bring the tension down a little, and I released the breath I was holding.

"Sorry, I get a little crazy when I think someone is hurting her," Xavier spoke as Mason's glare seemed to fall, and he nodded when I ran a hand across his arm. Bad enough we took the risk of being out in the front area of the club. I usually would be in our room, away from the crowd. But tonight, I wanted to try something different and watch a little before we sauntered off to be alone.

"Senator—" I raised my hand to cut her off. I didn't want anyone bringing up my name and causing any confusion.

"I like to keep my identity under wraps." I motioned around the room, and she smiled in acknowledgment. Mason started Club Seek as a place to get away and explore all your desires. When approved for membership, you were guaranteed discretion. Everyone signed a non-disclosure agreement during the vetting process. Having the price tag of fifty thousand to join came with significant perks from private drivers to and from the club.

"Sorry, I was just shocked to see you here," Chelsey said, and I waved her off.

"No worries, I need to get back to my evening. Please keep this between us, Chelsey," I said. She raised her hand and crossed her middle and index finger in gesture. I chuckled and walked off with Mason behind me. He placed his hand on my lower back and escorted me to our room as the live entertainment finished. Everyone mostly congregated to a corner or went to a room after getting a key.

"Who was that?" Mason questioned, placing his fingers on the lower part of my back and escorting me through the private area of Seek and down the hall to his room. I looked over my shoulder at Chelsey as she continued to explain the situation. As we approached the door, he leaned up against my back while sliding the key inside. His strong, musky aroma invaded my nose. I told myself this would be a one-time thing over and over again in my head, and now I looked at myself in the mirror and realized that lie wouldn't last any longer.

"Walk inside." His lips pressed against my shoulder. Feeling my stomach drop, I peered up, looking around the room.

I felt a chill run down my arm when he locked the door, knowing all my fantasies would come true tonight, and we'd both be in heaven from the games we liked to play. His large hands, wrapped around my stomach, held me in place. All my senses heightened with just his presence surrounding me. He decorated the room in brown and black trimming from the king-size bed, throw pillows, to the Picasso art piece hanging on the wall, to the silk robes he had custom-made with our initials. Our little getaway from the outside world, where I liked to escape and be Maya instead of Senator Hill.

"Pull the stress away." I covered my hand over his.

"Mmmmm… I want to kiss you, lick you, make you mine all

over again." Mason ran his hand up my chest, gripping my neck.

"I missed you." His left hand pulled the spaghetti strap down.

I moaned, "Ahhh… Prove it."

"Undress," Mason demanded as he stalked over to the bar in the corner and poured his usual glass of cognac and stared at me. Removing my dress slowly like he usually liked, I kept my heels on and swished over to the bed, peering over at him as he gave a curt nod.

"You've kept her away from me." Mason ran his finger around the rim of his glass, guzzling the last drop. Strolling to the dresser drawer across from the bed, he pulled out the feather, a small bullet vibrator.

"Am I being punished?" I questioned, raised my right brow.

"Tonight is about your pleasure. I can tell by your voice you can't handle anything else."

"Come here." I reached for his hand, letting him kiss the back of my palm. I scooted back in the bed against the head-board as he tossed the pillows on the floor.

"Touch yourself." Mason's husky voice echoed throughout the room, watching him remove his jacket, shoes, and shirt as I pulled my thong down. Gripping my left breast, I tweaked my nipple, licking my lips as we stared at each other. Seeing the lust in his eyes of what we were about to do only compelled me even more, pushing my right hand down to my stomach playing with my sex. Wetness dripped down my legs already before he could even touch me.

"Mason… Uhhhh." Goosebumps broke out, imagining his tongue gliding up my slit.

"You're stunning, Maya," Mason called out, leaning down and pressing kisses on my left and right ankle, up my leg to my inner thigh and teasing, avoiding my essence. Mason's large body hovered over me, capturing my mouth, dizzying me with his tongue. He gripped my hands, pushing them over my head.

"Mmmmm… Yes, baby," I moaned, squeezing my eyes tight. He held my arms up with one hand and pushed his index finger into my entrance.

"Are you ready to be pleased?" Arching off the bed, I bit his bottom lip and pulled back.

"Mason… Uhhhh," I moaned, wanting to taste myself on his lips.

"Don't move." He pecked me on the mouth again, removed his hands, and reached over for the feather, slowly caressing it across my heavy breasts, down to my stomach. Closing my eyes again, I savored the time we had together. I heard the buzz of the vibrator turn on and popped my eyes open. He hovered it over an inch away from my throbbing mound.

"Please," I groaned, opening my legs wider.

He held the vibrator against my clit, while sucking my dark nipples into his mouth. Squirming from the double intensity, I felt my chest rise, and my head tossed and turned, fighting the temptation to touch him back. My hips subconsciously rocked back and forth, and my eyes grew heavy.

"I need you now."

"Do you want to come, baby?" Mason asked me, using his tongue to penetrate the deepest core of my soul.

"Yes, please… Oh, God!" It was demanding, letting me know that no one would ever compare.

"Soon." Hearing the zipper of his pants, Mason paused, reaching to the nightstand for a condom. A long time ago, we agreed we didn't want any accidents separately from protecting against any diseases even though I wasn't seeing anybody else. Kids weren't in the plan for my future, with my schedule only growing.

Tapping his dick against me, I tried to grip his shaft, and he smacked my hand away.

"No touching, Senator Hill," Mason grunted, thrusting forward. Sweat beads dripped across my forehead. As the room spun, my eyes grew blurry from processing the overwhelming passion coming off his large body. Feeling his hands run through my hair, I tilted my head back.

* * *

Two hours later, the door was held open for me, and I walked away wearing my same clothes, feeling satisfied. The car pulled up for me to get inside. Tony started to open the door to come to help me, and I held my hand up to stop him.

"I got it."

A flash of light came across, and I looked around, trying to see where it was coming from. The security guard behind nudged me into the limo.

"Everything all right, Senator?" he said. I looked behind me, standing in the middle of the door with my leg halfway inside.

"Uh, yeah. I thought I saw something." I shook my head and got into the car, and Tony pulled off, staring through the back window. I tried searching the buildings and alleyways for the flash again.

Picking up my phone, I opened a text message thread, looking for Mason's name.

Me: Did you have security do a sweep tonight?

Mason: I always do a sweep.

Me: I think I was followed.

Mason: Are you sure you want to be alone?

I gnawed on my bottom lip.

Me: Tonight was great, but I need to work early in the morning.

Mason: All right, I want to see you soon.

Me: I'll get back to you.

Turning my phone off, I laid my head on the back of the seat, closing my eyes, wondering if my secret was out. This was the little peace I enjoyed where I could be myself and not a senator in demand for someone else. The car pulled up to the house, and Tony started to get out. I placed my hand on his shoulder.

"It's fine, Tony. I can make it from here."

"I'll wait out here to make sure you get inside comfortably."

Opening the door, I wave good night and head to the front door, sliding the key in my one-story, ten-thousand-square-foot home. Becoming a senator afforded me a nice, well-off place for my family to visit with three bedrooms, four baths.

I dropped my keys in the cup holder, kicking off my heels and coat. I jogged upstairs to my bedroom to end the night with a hot bath before work tomorrow.

CHAPTER 2

SENATOR HILL

The senate meeting finally finished, and I left the room and walked back to my office with my assistant next to me, still feeling the effects of a night out at Club Seek.

"Senator Hill, you have lunch with Congressman Dole today," Jennifer spoke, running down my calendar of events.

"Anything else major? I was trying to leave early today." I checked my watch as we approached the door to my office. She pushed it open, walked inside, and I headed to my desk. As she sat on her own, I noticed a large manila envelope addressed to me.

"A few calls with the local newspapers and then another meeting with the speaker of the house." Jennifer crossed her legs, briefing me on the day. I flipped the envelope open, removing the contents, raising my hand to my mouth in shock. There were pictures of me at Club Seek, one of me standing with the security guard and one of me laughing with Mason. There was even one of his bedroom with me dressed in lingerie.

"OMG." I dropped the pictures on the desk, jumping up and pacing back and forth.

Jennifer stood and hovered over the desk, grabbing the pictures.

"Who took these?" she asked.

Shaking my head, tears fell down my cheeks.

"I don't know."

"They didn't leave a note or anything. Do you have enemies?"

"I'm a senator. Enemies come with the territory."

"Maybe you should tell Mason." Jennifer picked up more pictures, glancing up at me.

"I don't know."

Turning to look out the window, I saw Tony standing in front of the limo, pointing at a photographer. They often came up to the capital to harass staff, and they knew him by name, which could lead me to feel that maybe he was behind this or Mason.

"What if this has Mason behind it?"

"You can't be serious. Mason loves you," Jennifer replied. A knock came at the door. Jennifer hurriedly put all the photos back in the envelope, passing them to me, and I slid them into my bottom cabinet.

"Come in!" I shouted, sitting at the desk and wiping tears away.

"Senator Hill, I think it's time we had a discussion about the bill you proposed," Congressman Kurt Jones said.

"Mr. Jones, we've debated, and you've made it clear where you stand."

"I'm inclined to change my mind."

"Why would you do that?"

He crossed his arms over his chest, his right brow lifted.

"Let's say I have an idea that you'll need my help down the road."

"What is that supposed to mean?" I jumped out of the chair, agitated that he may know of the pictures I was hiding. He raised his hands in the air, smiling.

"You'll never get your agenda passed. It's better to play nice now."

"Jennifer, will you please escort Congressman Jones out of my office?"

"No need, I have another meeting with the speaker in a half hour. Remember, I can put a good word in for you." Kurt winked, walking out of my office.

"He's disgusting," Jennifer said, heading to the office door.

"Can you hold all my calls for the next two hours? I need to figure out what's going on."

"You going to call Mason?" Jennifer inquired.

"I just hope this doesn't come back to haunt me."

I pulled my cell phone from my purse and dialed Mason's number. It went to voicemail, and I hung up and tried again.

"Where is he?" I muttered to myself, then decided to call my parents.

"Hey, Maya," Dad spoke.

"Hi, Dad. Where's Mom?"

Hearing something rustling on the other end, I pulled the phone away for a brief second.

"What are you doing?"

"I'm out working on my car. Your mother's at the store."

"Oh."

"What's wrong? Usually you don't call during this time of day."

"Nothing. I just missed you two."

"We miss you, but you're only a forty-five-minute drive away."

I chuckled, knowing he was right. I always counted on my dad to make me feel better about anything. Being an only child, it came with me as the apple of their eye. I was spoiled and treated like royalty growing up.

"Tell Mom I called, and I'll try to clear my schedule to have dinner later in the week."

"Are you sure everything is okay?"

"I'm fine, Dad. Call you later."

"All right. Love you, little girl," he said.

"Love you too, bye." We hung up at the same time. I sighed, sitting back in the chair, holding my hands up to my face. Whoever was behind these pictures was trying to destroy my life, and I refused to let my parents be hurt.

Jennifer strolled into the office, holding bags of food.

"Lunch is here, but the speaker wants to talk with you." She placed soup and a sandwich down.

"When did you talk to him?"

"While you were on the phone," Jennifer said.

"I don't have time for this, and I'm not hungry."

"You need to eat. Do you want me to make up a lie?"

"Yes... No... wait." I groaned, lifting the phone to see if Mason called or texted back.

"You know it's because of Jones that he wants to see you."

Nodding in agreement, I stood and grabbed my cell to head to his office. I figured it was better to find out what he wanted before things got even crazier.

"Hold my calls for the rest of the day. I doubt I'll be up to having another meeting when I get back."

"Try not to get yourself too stressed," Jennifer replied.

Pursing my lips, I checked my appearance before leaving, and Jennifer followed by shutting the door. Walking through the busy hallways, I scanned the crowds and got a feeling like someone was watching me. Shaking off the reaction, I continued to the elevator and waited with another few members as the doors opened. Stepping on a few seconds later, I punched the top level for his floor. Arriving five minutes later, I treaded over to his secretary's desk, motioning toward his open door.

"He's waiting for you," she said.

"Thanks."

Knocking on the door, he waved me in, and I closed the door behind me, strolling to the chair in front of his desk. His office always creeped me out, with the pictures of just him hanging on the wall; there was nothing with his wife or son.

"I wanted to meet with you about this proposal of yours." Adam held the early draft of my bill in his hands.

"What would you like to talk about?"

"Jones thinks you should scrap this for now, and I'm inclined to agree."

I pushed down my honest thoughts. Adam's bushy brows furrowed, and I glared right back at him.

"My agenda is to support my community."

"You will, under my leadership."

"I won't be silenced, and Kurt has no right to go behind my back."

"Do you know how laws get passed?" he asked.

"I'm not here to debate on my job, Mr. Speaker."

"Then you'll put this aside."

"Are you saying you won't bring it to the floor?"

"I'm saying I run things around here. Get with the program," he argued, throwing my bill in the trash can. I scoffed and stormed out of his office with a headache forming, smashing the down button to head back to my office. Stomping off the elevator toward my office, Jennifer waved a stack of messages in front of my face, and I snatched them out of her hand before pushing my door open and slamming it closed.

"Arghh!" I screamed, pacing back and forth.

"What happened?" Jennifer tapped on the door, pushing it open, not waiting to be called.

"Nothing."

"Maya, I can clearly see something happened."

"Kurt is what happened."

"Take the rest of the day off; you're not up to finishing any meetings."

"You're right. I have the worst headache." I hugged her, grabbing my purse and coat before passing back the messages, and leaving the office. While going toward the elevator, I saw Kurt and Adam talking in a huddle together. They were up to something, and I just needed to be prepared.

CHAPTER 3

MASON

$\mathcal{M}$orris knocked on my office door, strolling in with a hard grimace on his face. He was a silent partner in Club Seek, and with him being a security agent, I was able to leverage a lot of his clients to join the club.

"She's pissing me off."

"Who?" I finished signing off on inventory for the club.

"Lisa." Morris unbuttoned his jacket, standing with his hands on top of the chair in front of the desk. When Maya told me about her friend Lisa, I wasn't as forthcoming with inviting her in as she was. She was well known, and the lightest slip could hurt not only my business, but Maya's career. Her job in the media was a big no for me and my business. My clients trusted that I could keep their privacy from being revealed, which was the reason I had strict requirements on my contracts.

Leaning back in my seat with my hands clasped together in my lap, I could see the veins clearly in Morris' forehead.

"Tell me something new; it seems like every week you two are fighting."

"She refuses to take security when she comes and goes."

"Has something happened?" I needed to know if Maya was in jeopardy. Even though being a senator, she was equipped with her own security, I preferred to have my own people with her at all times.

"No, Lisa just thinks I'm overprotective."

I shrugged my shoulders, chuckling to myself.

"What's so funny?"

"I hear the same thing from Maya."

He came around and sat in the chair, propping his arm on the desk.

"At least with Maya, you're able to get her to understand."

"Lisa's headstrong. You might need to go easy on her."

"The last thing she needs is me going easy on her."

"Well, I have my own problems."

"Your dad or Maya this time?"

I shuffled the papers on my desk.

"He wants me to come work for him and quit this little frat boy work," I scoffed, thinking over our last conversation in my head.

"He's still on that same argument?"

I nodded, sighing with a hand running down my face.

"Doesn't matter that I have multiple businesses and am doing fine without using his connections."

"Sounds like you have just as many problems as me."

"Yeah, you want a drink?" I pointed, standing and strolling toward the bar in the corner of my office. Lifting the top from the brown scotch, I filled the cup halfway, passing it toward him and filling the second glass for myself.

"Thanks," he said.

Placing one hand in my pocket, I tilted my head back, gulping the drink down. Squeezing my eyes shut, I let the warm, subtle notes drain down my throat.

"I need another one."

"Keep drinking, you're never going to be ready for Maya."

"She's not coming tonight. We're supposed to meet for dinner," I replied.

Morris held his glass out for another shot, lowering his eyes toward his watch.

"I have to run. I called a meeting with my team before I came here." He stood, handing me the glass.

"Let me know if you're able to run point next week," I said.

"Sure will."

"Try not to run yourself crazy over Lisa."

Morris waved me off, walking out of the office, and I finished off my second drink, sitting back down in my chair, looking over last-minute emails.

When my phone rang, I groaned at someone disturbing me during my downtime. I picked up the phone, hearing my father's secretary on the other end.

"Please hold for Mr. Norris," Sheila said.

A part of me wanted to hang up, but he would just have her call me right back.

"Mason," my father said.

"Sir."

Adam Norris was the type of person who only looked out for himself. Growing up, if I didn't follow the rules, I would basically be seen as the piranha of our family. All my cousins followed in the family business of politics, and I strayed toward business, then owning a few clubs that happened to cater to people's sexual needs. My father only told them I was the owner of a few restaurants, which was true, but he left the part of Club Seek from my resume.

"What do you need?"

Massaging my temples, I stayed silent, waiting to hear what new request he had for me.

"I'm having a little fundraiser at the house."

"I can't."

"You will. Your mother hasn't talked to you in a while."

"Why? Not like you're going to introduce me to anyone."

"Because I said to come. You don't think I have the power to end your little business?"

There's the Adam Norris I knew very well.

"Threatening your son?" My brow lifted in surprise.

He cleared his throat.

"Mason, this is important. Put our differences aside," he said.

"Send the details to me, and I'll see if I can make it," I said, hanging up, not waiting for him to respond. Shaking my head, I sent off some more emails and decided it was time to end the day and meet up with Maya for dinner.

* * *

I OPENED the door to the Spartine, an Italian restaurant not too far from my house, and the hostess seated me right away since I was a frequent guest.

"Two tonight, Mr. Norris?"

"Yes. She should be here soon."

Sara placed the menus down on the table, and I grabbed my phone from my pocket to check my messages. I saw Jameson and my mother texted me, but nothing from Maya.

Jameson: The order of liquor came in.

Catherine: Son, I'm glad you're coming.

Me: Where are you?

Me: Did you get my message about dinner?

"Well, look who stumbled into my little world."

I lifted my head up, smirking at Erica Brownstone, actress and former fling of mine. Standing next to the empty chair, she bit her bottom lip.

"Erica."

"Mason, don't tell me you're eating alone." Erica leaned over the table, running her palm across my shoulder. I backed up so her hand would fall off and get the hint as the waitress came up to my table. Erica Brownstone never had a problem with showing off, and today was no different. Out of the many years we'd known each other, she always wanted more from me. The problem was that she was extremely self-absorbed and wanted all the attention on her.

"I'm actually waiting for someone."

"Really? Maybe I can keep you company until she gets here." Erica sat without me inviting her.

"Are you ready to order, sir?"

"I'd love a glass of white wine," Erica said.

Glancing at my phone again, I didn't see a response from Maya.

"Anything for you, sir?"

"Um… I'll have the same thing." As I placed my phone in my pocket, Erica smiled, tossing her hair back.

"So, are you seeing anyone?" Erica questioned.

"I saw a commercial for your latest movie. You looked good," I said, trying to change the subject. She laughed, taking a sip of water.

"Come on, Mason, we used to be able to talk and be friendly."

"True, but now you're a big star. I'd hate for any rumors to get out."

"Some rumors can be helpful." Erica extended her hand, rubbing across my palm. Removing my hand from her reach, Erica looked around the room, likely to see if anyone saw the rejection. Our waitress came back with our drinks, and I thanked her, letting Erica order a meal.

"Listen, it's good seeing you, Erica, but I have to go," I said, attempting to stand.

"Wait! It's just dinner, Mason," Erica pouted.

"Dinner that I was expecting to have with someone else."

"Do you love her?"

"I'm not answering that."

"Well, she's a lucky girl."

"Have a good night," I said, treading out and stopping at the bar to tell the bartender to put her meal on my account. My next mission was finding out why Maya never showed up tonight.

CHAPTER 4

SENATOR HILL

"**A**rghhhh!!!" My wrist tightened against the cuffs as the second strike came across my ass, clenching my teeth, and my body continued to be dominated by the flogger. I ignored his calls yesterday, consumed with work, and we'd promised ourselves that would never happen. Even though I wanted to tell him what was going on, I wanted to let the night be about us only and leave work outside these walls.

He peppered kisses against my spine, leaning in behind with his chest to my back. I wanted to touch and taste him in my mouth.

"Maya, you drive me crazy," he murmured, running his hands all over my body.

"I want to taste you," I begged.

"Not tonight. You lost that luxury."

I gasped, pumping in, feeling him in my stomach. My breath caught in my throat.

"You understand what this is about?"

Nodding my head, I knew he was pushing my boundaries and challenging me to disagree, but I wouldn't because this was both of us becoming as one. He couldn't deny me for too long, hearing his groans and grunts of satisfaction. Our mouths parted in whimpers, hearing his moans next to my ear. Gripping my hips, Mason pulled out and sucked on my pussy, sliding his one finger into my asshole.

"Mason!" I trembled under his touch. The entire bed was soaking wet from juices and combined sweat. I tensed up, feeling the tingling rise, wanting to beg for a release.

"Please, baby, can I come!" I screamed, yanking against the cuffs again.

All of a sudden, he drew back his finger and tongue, sliding his dick back in, pumping faster, leaving me on edge.

"Arghh… Fuck, Maya, come for me!" Mason shouted, reaching around and playing with my clit. I squirted on command, shaking beneath the restraints. All I wanted to do was fall asleep in his arms.

"Relax, I'm not going anywhere." I heard, a few seconds later, a warm towel wiping me clean.

"I love you," I mumbled slowly.

"I'm still upset with you."

He pulled me into his arms.

"I was upset after talking with your father," I confessed.

Mason cupped my chin, staring into my eyes.

"What happened?" he asked.

I moved out of his hold and adjusted to sit up against the headboard.

"He won't move forward with the bill I co-wrote. Plus. I think he's working to destroy my career."

"Explain."

"I don't want to put you in the middle of my problems." I started to get out of the bed, and Mason gripped me around the waist.

"Tell me, Maya."

"I need to get in line with what he wants, or I need to look for a career to end."

"Son of a bitch," Mason grunted, tossing the sheet off his body, reaching for his boxers and pants.

"Wait! What are you doing?" I crawled toward the end of the bed.

"I'm going to talk to him."

"No! Mason, this is my problem."

"He's my father, and no one threatens you," Mason demanded.

Shaking my head, I stepped off the bed, wrapping the sheet around my body. Capturing Mason's arm, I turned him toward me.

"I understand, but please let me handle him."

"Maya," Mason groaned, pulling me into his chest.

"Please, it will only make things worse."

"I'll let you handle it for now, but I can't promise."

"Thank you."

"I want you to come as my date."

"To what?"

Going out in public wasn't our thing. Seeing things change as we got closer caused an unexpected flutter in my heart.

"A fundraiser."

"Fundraiser?" I pried, watching him lean down and peck my lips.

"Nothing major."

"Ummm… huh."

"Are you coming to my place tonight?"

Reaching down to grab my dress and shoes, I went to the bathroom to get redressed, leaving the door halfway open.

"I have so much work."

"Maya, you keep pushing me away, and you think I don't notice."

"Mason, you're overreacting," I said, running my hands through my hair.

"After last night when you stood me up. I decided this was moving forward." He pointed between him and me.

"Who made you in charge of deciding my life?"

He stood in the middle of the doorway of the bathroom, still shirtless with his muscles on display, begging for my tongue to taste every square corner of his broad chest.

"I did. Because we both know that you love everything I do to you." He stalked in slow toward me, reaching out to caress my cheek.

"May I suggest you be patient with me?"

"You can suggest, but we both know you like it when I take control." Mason smacked me on the butt, squeezing both cheeks, making me moan in anticipation of another round in bed together.

"I do love you, though."

"Show me."

"Another time. I have work to do," I said, standing on my tiptoes, pressing a kiss to his lips.

"You can work at my place." Mason pulled back, letting me out of the bathroom first, following after.

"Okay, and you can tell me more about this fundraiser."

Friday afternoon.

I sat with Jennifer at lunch, going over my schedule for the week at Spartine, debating on what else I could do to handle Mason's father without causing a rift between them.

"I have you scheduled for back-to-back calls," Jennifer said.

"Who are they with?"

"A few senators and small business owners."

"Try to make them all in one day."

"I got your dress for the fundraiser with Mason."

"Did he finally send the information over?"

"That's what I wanted to confirm with you."

Lifting the fork, I pushed pasta around on my plate.

"What do you mean?"

"Adam Norris' fundraiser," Jennifer remarked.

I choked on my food, coughing as she passed the glass of water over to me.

"Are you sure?"

"Yes." She passed her phone over to me. I looked at her email exchange with Mason, seeing the time, date, and specifics.

"I told him I didn't want to deal with him."

"Do you want me to cancel?"

I started to answer when I saw a flash of light go off, and the door opened as a woman walked inside with a crowd of people surrounding her.

"No, I already said I would go."

I went back to eating my food when I heard a voice call out my name.

"Maya Hill, right?" the woman amongst the entourage called my name. Wearing large shades, I figured she was someone important.

"Yes."

She held her hand out toward me. I reached over and gave her a shake.

"Erica Brownstone, we have something in common."

"I doubt we have anything in common."

"Oh… really… hmmm, I guess Mason didn't tell you about our dinner date."

I yanked my hand back.

"No worries, he's mysterious like that," Erica said.

"How do you know Mason?"

"We go way back. Surprised he's never spoken about our relationship," Erica replied.

"Yeah, really surprised."

"Well, I'll let you get back to your lunch. Tell Mason I'll call him soon." Erica winked, swishing her hips before heading to her friends. They sat in the booth giggling at the performance she had just put on, and I rolled my eyes. Jennifer snapped her fingers.

"That's Erica Brownstone; she's an actress."

"She needs more training because she's terribly dramatic." Jennifer laughed.

"I remember seeing a movie with her not too long ago."

"At least she dresses better than she acts."

"You think Mason's dating her too?

"I don't know, but I plan on finding out."

"In the meantime, try to focus on what you're going to do about the speaker."

"Maybe going to dinner wouldn't be so bad," I muttered, cupping my chin with my elbow on the table. I'd been playing things too easy with everyone, to the point they felt like I was a pushover.

"Seeing the gleam in your eyes, I can only imagine," Jennifer responded, taking a bite of her baked ziti.

"I need to gather more information, but I'm not letting them run me out of Congress."

* * *

HE RAN a hand down my chest, across my stomach, and over my navel, dipping his middle finger in my warm canal. After work, he surprised me at my place and brought dinner. Before I could even talk with him about the fundraiser or Erica, I was tied up against the headboard with my legs spread open, with his tongue and fingers exploring. Feeling his smooth, warm palm move in and out at a slow pace drove me insane. It was all about his plan to tease me and push me to the cliff. As tired as I was at first, this brought new life into my blood.

"Are you ready?"

"Mmmmm…"

My hair was out of the normal ponytail, fanned around my pillow. I looked up with wide eyes as he cupped the side of my face. He recaptured my lips, sliding his tongue inside. He pressed his hard body against my skin. I was panting, groaning, wanting to feel him take me again.

"Yesss…"

"You are so beautiful, baby."

Snaking his tongue to lick my nipple, it was intoxicating and frustrating, wanting to touch him but unable to wrap my arms around his neck. I arched my back a little, moving my hips and feeling aroused.

"I want to feel you."

"You will, in time."

CHAPTER 5

SENATOR HILL

The next day, it was finally Sunday. The bright sun was shining, and I wore my shades sitting in the backseat, looking over the text from Mason. Right now, he was texting to set another date, and I didn't know if I would be able to get time off with the upcoming schedule. Whenever we had our meetups and I left, I still craved his presence.

Mason: Are you still thinking about me?

Me: Always.

Mason: Come see me.

Me: I can't, meeting with my friends.

Mason: Afterwards, what are you doing?

The car stopped, and Tony opened the door and stepped out to help escort me inside.

"Thanks, Tony. I can ride home with Lisa. Take the afternoon off."

"Senator—"

"I'll be fine, Tony, don't worry."

"I'll feel better if I stick around." Tony released a breath, shutting the door and leading me in toward the backroom. The hostess nodded at me, and I smiled, never looking around at the other guests. We continued toward the private dining area, and Tony slid the doors open to reveal Lisa, Kyla, and Chelsey sitting and laughing.

"Tony!" all three blurted out excitedly, and Tony blushed. All my friends flirted with Tony whenever he came around them. I could admit he was tall, dark, handsome, protective, and loyal.

"Finally, the queen has made her presence known." Lisa giggled, holding up her glass of mimosa. We'd been friends since freshman year of college, and she was a TV anchor. Kyla, the youngest of our group, was a well-known actress filming a movie in town. So, it was extra special when she came to visit. Normally, she lived in New York. Our friendship came about from Lisa when she interviewed her at a movie premiere. Then Chelsey was new to our group, but I felt a connection from the first time I deposited money with her family's bank.

"Ladies," Tony said, shaking his head at them.

"Thanks, Tony." He pulled the chair out for me, and I sat, placing my phone and purse down on the table. My phone vibrated, and I quickly remembered Mason texting me.

"Oops, someone's in trouble," Lisa said.

"Ohhh." Kyla and Chelsey chuckled.

Mason: Will I see you later?

Me: Sorry, I was talking with the girls. I'll call you when I leave.

Mason: Don't forget, Maya.

Me: I won't.

Mason: If you do, punishment of my tongue is coming.

I squeezed my legs together and bit my bottom lip, flashing back to the last time I disobeyed him, and I was deprived of his tongue, watching him come in front of me without letting me touch him.

Lisa snapped her fingers in front of my face.

"Tell Mason you're busy, and you'll ride his tongue later," Lisa joked, slapping hands with Kyla.

A crooked grin came across my face. I placed the phone down, searching all three of their eyes.

"Have you ordered yet?" I inquired. Right as the doors opened, trays of food were placed on the table. The restaurant served everything from Italian, soul food, breakfast items, to steak and seafood. Lisa's boyfriend knew the owner, so the atmosphere was casual but expensive. They catered to a lot of high-profile customers on the weekends.

"Yes, and I'm starving," Chelsey replied, picking up her fork and digging into her vegetable omelet. Today would be the best time to talk about the incident at the club since Mason and Xavier hadn't met officially.

"I hear you and Mason are together now," Kyla said, passing her empty glass over to the server.

"We just agreed a few days ago."

"So it's serious between you two?"

Lisa's black hair hung loosely out of her everyday updo she wore on air, with her deep-set brown eyes standing out to her yellowish-brown skin tone. Each of us was different, and most people wondered how we became friends. Lisa was the most outgoing. Kyla was the strongest, ready to fight out battles. I was considered the mother of the bunch, and Chelsey was the quieter one.

"Too early to tell."

"Chelsey told us about Xavier and Mason," Kyla mentioned. I stared, trapped by her smoky, warm, bronze skin tone. Her mother was Haitian and Hispanic, and her father was Jamaican. Lisa nicknamed her Babydoll because she looked like a doll with her big, wide eyes, button nose, and high cheekbones.

"Xavier's just overprotective," Chelsey told us and I nodded, understanding having the type of guy who was overprotective of his woman.

"All men get like that at some point."

"I'm going to meet Morris there tonight," Lisa explained.

"Have you been invited yet, Kyla?" Chelsey questioned.

"No, doubt I have time with my schedule," Kyla answered, her dreadlocks lined against her oval-shaped face.

"Mason owns the place, Maya. You take Kyla," Lisa suggested, biting into her pancakes, revealing her devilish smile.

"I have to check my schedule. You know what I'm dealing with in Congress."

"How is everything at work?" Chelsey pushed loose strands of her bouncy hair behind her ear. The glossy lipstick covered her full lips.

"Stressful. I'm trying to push my agenda and get things going."

"Don't let it discourage you."

"Let's make a toast."

"To what?"

"Toast to us for being boss women." Lisa raised her glass up, and we cheered, taking a sip.

AN HOUR LATER, I put my shades on, heading out behind Lisa and Tony covering me as much as possible. People often stopped me to start a conversation on some issue they were dealing with. When I was dressed down, I liked to not be noticed if I didn't need to be. Tony pushed the doors open, and a swarm of photographers and reporters yelled, shoving microphones in my face.

"Senator Hill! Senator Hill!" reporters yelled.

"Back up. Back up!" Tony replied, pushing through the crowd, holding onto my hand. I usually didn't have a huge group surrounding me and wondered what the issue was this time. Reporters kept a distance sometimes, but this was insane with over twenty people surrounding my town car.

"We need to leave," Tony said.

"What happened?" I asked. He reached for the door, and I started to get inside when someone shoved a picture in front of my face.

"Is this you, Senator Hill?" a reporter asked. I pushed her hand away and jumped inside my car. Tony shut the door, not waiting to see if any of the girls were able to leave through the massive crowd.

"Check your phone," he replied, starting the car, honking his horn as the audience grew bigger with cell phones out, filming us.

"This is nuts," I muttered, opening my phone and seeing nonstop messages and missed calls.

"Senator, call me ASAP," Jennifer said, with an attached photo of me dressed in lingerie with Mason holding a flogger behind me.

"Oh My God!" I shouted.

SENATOR HILL

I shut the TV off from another reporter telling people how much of a disappointment I was, pacing back and forth in front of Mason, Jennifer, and Chelsey. I shook my head, feeling on the brink of breaking down in tears. My entire career was plastered online with people making comments about how I shouldn't be in public office. I loved my job and wanted to make a difference in the world. I never expected that what I did in private would cause so much backlash. I'd been at Mason's house since everything happened, taking calls and meetings over the phone. Even Jennifer got pulled into my problems with people hounding her family. Kyla and Lisa messaged me and wanted to come to check on me, but I declined, not wanting any more spotlight on me. Bad enough reporters were camped out down the street from Mason's house. It was so bad, Kyla had to take a few days off from the news station because they wanted her to report on the news, and she felt a conflict of interest.

"My life is ruined."

"Don't say that, Maya," Chelsey replied, walking over and placing her hand on her back.

"I knew this was a mistake." I balled my fist up, wanting to scream.

"What did you say?" Mason called out.

I wasn't up for fighting with him.

"Mason, please let's not do this right now." I raised my hand, stopping him from coming any closer.

"No, I think this is the time to get some things straight." He reached for my hand, and I tried to turn away.

"Maybe we should grab some food," Jennifer spoke, standing up with her purse and keys.

"That won't be necessary," I said.

"Jennifer, take all the time you need," Mason remarked, making me roll my eyes at him trying to control everything.

"I know a great barbeque place," Chelsey said, hugging me.

"All right, take Tony," I demanded, wanting to make sure they were protected.

Chelsey nodded, leaving with Jennifer. Pushing Mason away, I stomped off to the kitchen, needing fresh air.

"I can't believe you," I huffed, pointing at him.

"Listen to me, Maya."

"Mason, you don't understand what this means for my career." I threw my hands in the air.

"I get it, baby, but you're pushing the wrong person away."

"Maybe coming here was a mistake."

He gripped my chin, forcing eye contact, pressing his chest to mine.

"I don't give a damn what the newspaper or online says. This is not a mistake."

I jerked out of his hold.

"Because your father is Adam Norris, you never have to deal with anything!" I shouted, regretting the words when they left my mouth.

"I've heard that same thing over and over my entire life but never expected you of all people."

I extended a hand out to him.

"Mason…"

He shook me off.

"If this is too much, I won't fight you on leaving." Mason marched out of the kitchen.

Standing alone, I felt the weight of the world falling in on me. I heard the door open, then close, and I jumped up, running to see where he was going.

"Mason! Mason!"

Jumping in his car, he drove off and didn't look back. Before I ran toward his car backing out of the driveway, a swarm of reporters accosted me.

"Senator Hill! Is it true you're resigning?"

"Senator Hill! Are you a prostitute?"

"Senator Hill! Senator Hill!"

Nonstop questions and cameras hit me in my face, I pushed through the crowd, running back inside. Upstairs in his bedroom, I hid under the covers, crying over the end of my relationship with Mason.

* * *

FOUR HOURS LATER, I felt strong arms around me lying in bed, sniffing from my earlier tears. I tried to turn around in bed, but he wouldn't let me.

"No."

"I'm sorry."

He sighed, kissing the back of my neck.

"I know."

"Please don't leave me."

"You're making it hard."

"What can I do?"

Squeezing me close, he loosened his hold, letting me adjust so we were face to face. The back of his palm ran down my cheek.

"Stop fighting me. My father is more than likely behind this."

I tried to sit up, but he forced me back down, kissing me on the lips.

"How do you know?"

"I went to see him."

"Wait, are you serious?"

Mason turned, lying on his back.

"Adam Norris is controlling. He would do anything to keep me under his thumb, and I refuse."

"So he's trying to ruin my career."

"Pretty much."

"Bastard."

"The best way to get him to stop is to play fire with fire."

"That's not me, Mason."

"Maya, do you trust me?" Mason questioned.

"Yes."

"Then let things play out. Let me handle this for you." Mason rolled over, wrapping his arm around my waist.

"What about Erica?"

A hard grimace crossed his face.

"She's more than likely getting paid."

"I agree."

I recalled her doing an interview about how Mason was only using me to get his business funded since I was a senator and had connections. Obviously, Adam wanted to make Mason seem weak in public so he could crawl to him and get a job.

"I forgot we bumped into her at the restaurant."

"Jennifer told me while you were asleep," Mason informed me.

"Did Tony take them home?" I asked.

"No, they're still downstairs."

"What?"

"They didn't want to leave you alone, so we let you sleep."

"Let me go downstairs and tell them to head home."

He moved back, letting me out of bed. I pecked him on the lips again, holding his hand while we strolled down the stairs to see them watching a movie together.

"You look a little better," Jennifer said.

"I needed rest."

"We left you some food in the microwave," Chelsey said.

"Thank you, but I'm not hungry. I just want to thank you both."

"You don't have to thank us," Jennifer replied.

Letting go of Mason's hand, I walked around the couch to sit between them.

"I do. Everything is upside down, but you've been supportive beyond words."

"Well, your friends are here no matter what." Chelsey reached over to grip my hand.

"What's the plan? Are we beating Erica's ass?" Jennifer blurted out, and all three of us burst into laughter.

"I have more than enough problems. Having friends in jail for fighting wouldn't work."

Jennifer's bottom lip poked out, crossing her arms over her chest.

"For now, Mason will handle things because his father is behind everything."

Chelsey and Jennifer's eyes rose wide in shock.

"Speaker Norris?" Jennifer said.

"Wow." Chelsey shook her head in disbelief.

"Maybe doing an interview would help," Jennifer suggested.

"You don't think it would lead to more unnecessary harassment," Chelsey asked.

"Right now, I'm going to eat and head to bed."

"All right, keep me updated." Jennifer stood. I followed, walking her to the door along with Chelsey. Shutting the door,

I stared out the window, watching them leave with Tony. Mason came in front of me, picking me up bridal style and carrying me back to his bedroom. He helped me out of my clothes and took me into the bathroom. Putting me on the counter, he turned the water on in the tub. He kissed the top of my forehead and left me alone.

"Relax, and I'll be out here."

Smiling back at him, I nodded, stepping down and getting in the tub. I leaned back, closed my eyes, and prayed things would go away.

CHAPTER 7

MASON

Two days later.

I was standing at the door of my parents' home, with Maya on my arm. It was the night of the fundraiser for his campaign. Maya had been camping out at my place for the past few days because the reporters and photographers were constantly following her around when she went to work. Talking her into even coming tonight was an argument, but I promised we wouldn't stay long. I wanted to see how people were kissing my dad's ass just to get a leg up on any deals. Remembering the conversation we had the afternoon I stormed out on Maya played in my mind all night.

Flashback.

Arriving at my parents' house, I parked and jumped out of the car, not waiting for the butler to let my father know I was here. I slammed the door, stomping toward his office, the only room he stayed in most of the time. He was on a call, and I jerked it out of his hand and hung up.

"Mason, that was an important call."

"I don't know who you paid off but fix it now." I picked up the phone, holding it toward him.

"What are you talking about?" he questioned.

"Are we playing stupid now?"

"Listen, I'm your father, young man," he argued, pointing at me.

"Old man, I let you get away with a lot of things, but this is where I draw the line." He glanced away.

"Who do you think you're talking to?" He rose out of his seat.

"A man I thought wasn't so fucking greedy to hurt his son." He chuckled.

"Her pussy must really be good for you to talk to me this way."

I balled my fist up and punched him in the jaw. The door flew open, and my mother ran in, looking between us.

"Mason! What did you do?" She pushed me aside and went to my father.

"Get the hell out of my house!" he yelled.

"I know you paid somebody to take a photo of Maya."

"That little bitch is only after your money," he spat. Mother helped him up off the floor, and I tried to hit him again. She stood between us.

"Mason, stop it! What is this all about?" she asked.

My mother was naive to the dealings of my father and stayed more focused on her image and keeping up appearances.

"Your husband can explain."

"Adam, what is he talking about?" she said.

"Catherine, stay out of this," he said.

"I'm telling you right now, either you fix this, or I'll make your life a living hell."

"You will not speak to your father that way," she responded.

"Tell Mother how you paid a photographer to stalk Maya." My nostrils flared, and my chest heaved up and down. I was ready to beat his ass and go to jail if need be.

"Adam, please, whatever you've done, end it now," Mother pleaded.

"She's a liability, Mason," Dad remarked, sitting back down in his chair.

"Why? Because you can't have her under your thumb like a puppet?" I hissed.

"Damage our family name with those clubs and now sleeping with a woman who has no morals," he said, grabbing the napkin from my mother's hand and wiping the remnants of the blood off. I bent down, staring him in the eye.

"Fix this now, or you'll never see me again," I demanded, walking away as my father called my name.

* * *

PRESENT.

Running my palm across Maya's lower back, I kissed her shoulder blade as people stared at us. I held her hand, heading into the ballroom of the massive twenty-thousand-square-foot home I grew up in. Adam Norris was the son of Jimmy Norris, my grandfather and a politician who forced all of his kids to follow in his footsteps. I wanted normalcy, so I did my best not to go to a private school like my friends and be a normal kid. Now looking like the black sheep of the family, I had to deal with every judgment.

"Are you okay?" Maya asked, stopping us from walking further into the room.

"Just hard coming back here." I looked around the room, reminiscing on all the parties I had to attend when I was younger.

"I can just imagine with a father like Adam."

"Did I tell you how beautiful you looked?"

I tugged her into my arms, staring at her red lips that I wanted to taste. We hadn't been back to the club, let alone had sex with everything going on. I understood because we'd been distracted by having to deal with the public opinions everywhere we went. The other day, I tried to take her to dinner, and Tony had to keep her in the limo and turn around to head back home from all of the reporters camping outside the restaurant. I had no clue they knew we'd be there, other than someone at the restaurant calling the media.

"No, you haven't."

"I like this dress. Did Jennifer pick this out?"

She glanced down at the off-white, single-strapped dress that wrapped around her neck. Her curves poked out in the right places, causing my dick to strain in my pants. "Yes, I told her you'd be very happy with the choices," Maya said, fixing my bow tie.

"Maybe we can cut out now," I joked.

Maya giggled, shaking her head.

"Son, I'm glad you came," Dad said, glaring at Maya.

I pulled Maya in tighter on my side.

"I came here for one reason," I responded.

"Mason, please, we're having a party, son. All of that foolishness can wait." Mother waved at a few friends.

"Can we get a photo of the family together?" A photographer approached.

Maya started to walk away, and I pulled her in front of me.

"Immediate family," Dad told me.

"She's my family," I replied through clenched teeth.

"Mason, it's okay," Maya said.

"See, even she knows," Mom remarked, keeping a fake smile on her face.

"As of right now, I'm no longer family." I leaned over and pecked my mother's cheek, turning to leave the party.

"Adam, fix this right now!" Mother shouted.

"Catherine, be quiet," he fussed.

We strolled out of the ballroom through the hallway, gripping Maya's hand. I wanted to go back and punch my father in the face again but thought against it with so much media here tonight.

"Mason!" Erica yelled.

My head glanced to the left at my name being called, and I groaned, seeing Erica coming from the bathroom.

"Great," Maya grimaced, dropping my hand and trying to leave. I pulled her back to my side, kissing the side of her face.

"Why haven't you returned any of my calls?" Erica interrogated me, ignoring Maya.

"Why would I do that?" I quizzed, not up for her manipulating the situation. She knew what Maya was dealing with and probably worked with my father to destroy her career.

"We both know this won't last," Erica muttered.

"Girl!" Maya started to charge at Erica, and I tightened my hold, pushing her behind me.

"Not here," I whispered in her ear.

"Let me go," Maya demanded.

"Promise you won't hit her," I mumbled so she would only hear me.

She nodded in understanding. I released her and looked back at Erica.

"Erica, our time was over a long time ago. Move on."

"You don't mean that." Erica closed the space between us.

"Step one more foot toward him and find out what happens," Maya spoke.

"Adam Norris probably paid you a lot of money, but he can't save you from her," I told her.

Erica pursued her lips, glaring at Maya and taking a step back.

"He promised to finance my film project if I helped break you up," Erica confessed.

"What!" Maya gasped, covering her mouth in shock.

"Mason, please come back into the party." Mother came from around the corner with my father. My body heated up, and I charged toward him and punched him in the face, hearing loud gasps and screams of surprise. His security came over and pulled me off. I jerked away, pulling Maya with me.

"I'm done with you." I marched out of their home and helped Maya into the limo, then Tony sped away.

CHAPTER 8

SENATOR HILL

Sitting with my legs wide open, laying on the couch, I felt the tip of his dick against my lips, wanting entrance. I ran one hand down my torso, dipping my index finger between my folds, using my left hand to grip him in place. Licking from under the base of his balls, I pressed a kiss on the tip twice, fully taking him down my throat.

"Damn it, Maya!" His eyes narrowed.

"I believe you."

Seeing the way I had him almost ready to come undone, I removed my hand from my pussy and pushed toward his lips. He sucked my finger at the same time as I felt him thrust up in my mouth. Our moans grew louder and louder.

"Baby, make love to me," I whispered, popping him out of my mouth.

"Turn over."

Nodding in answer, I maneuvered on the couch with my back to his chest and felt his hands roam around my body.

"Stop teasing me."

Feeling his chest against my back, he grabbed my waist tight, placing kisses across my back, up to my neck and ear.

Gripping both breasts, I felt him thrusting inside, taking me off guard, and pushing through my walls.

"Ahhh…"

"Never doubt my love for you," Mason demanded, pulling my arms behind my back and pumping faster. Panting from the sensations of his touch, his gasps came in short spurts. Feeling his delicious thick member caused a tingling all over my body.

"Please…" I cried out.

My head spun as he released my arms, and I fell over the couch as his body fell on top of mine. Surrounding my clit with his finger, he tightened his right hand around my neck, biting my ear.

"I'm here, baby," he said, making me feel warm as the orgasms rolled around.

I whimpered, feeling heat wash over my face. Trembling in his hold, Mason slid out of me, turning around and making me straddle him.

"You're mine." He thrust up, never taking his eyes off me. I leaned back, caressing his balls and rotating my hips. Smacking my ass, I rode Mason until we were on the edge of a cliff.

"Fuck, you're sexy like this, baby," Mason said.

"Ohh… Yes…" I gasped.

"Sweetheart, I'm about to come."

"Come in me," I whimpered, tightening my thighs around his dick.

He growled, stroking faster, playing with my clit, with sweat seeping down our bodies.

"Ughh… Fuck! Maya," he cried out, pulling me into his chest, demanding my tongue.

I moaned into his mouth, pulling back and resting on top of his chest, exhausted and hot. Rubbing my butt slowly, he kissed the top of my head, and I drifted off to sleep.

* * *

Two hours later, I woke up in bed alone in the dark. I yawned, stretching my arms. I pulled the covers back and stepped out of bed. Taking the robe off the back of the door, I slid my feet in slippers and headed downstairs, looking around for Mason. I checked the kitchen, then his office without a trace. Sauntering out back toward the pool, I saw him sitting with a glass in his hand. I slid the door open and stepped outside, keeping the robe closed tight, wondering how long he had been out here.

"Hey," I said, sitting across from him on the chair.

"Sorry, I didn't mean to wake you."

"You know I only sleep if you're near me."

I stood from the chair and straddled his lap, taking the glass out of his hand and guzzling it down.

"Eww …" He patted my chest from tasting the sour scotch he loved so much. He chuckled, lifting his hands on my hips.

"Can't handle scotch." Mason pressed a kiss on my chest.

"Gross."

"I didn't want to wake you up."

"You talked to your parents?" I wondered.

Mason looked off.

"My mother tried calling, but I didn't answer."

"Maybe Jennifer's idea of me doing an interview would help."

"No." He tried to lift me off his lap.

"Wait! Just listen."

"Nothing to discuss."

"Baby, I hear you, but I would control the questions."

"Things will blow over."

"It's been almost a week."

"Fine, but I'm going with you," Mason said.

"I never doubted you wouldn't." I laughed. He picked me up with my legs wrapped around him.

"What are you doing? Mason, put me down."

He grinned, walking toward the pool. I tried to get down, and he tightened his grip.

"No, Mason!" He dropped in the pool with me in his arms. I came up for air pissed off, trying to catch my breath.

"Ughh! You asshole!" I splashed the water at him.

Mason chuckled, swimming toward me, pulling me into his chest.

"I love you," Mason said.

I pulled my hair into a bun, pushing him away.

"Asshole." I kissed him on the lips.

We decided to order food and watch a movie. I showered, dried my hair, and emailed Jennifer to set up an interview with Lisa. The public would hear the truth and hopefully cut Adam Norris off at the knees.

* * *

THE NEXT DAY, I knocked on the door of Chelsey's office. I waited for her permission to come in when I heard whispering. A few seconds later, the door opened with a stern glare on Xavier's face.

"Did I interrupt something?" I tried to hold in my laugh, but it was hard with his eyes staring a hole in Chelsey's direction. Obviously, they were doing something they shouldn't have been or probably often got away with, like Mason and me in his office.

"No, you didn't interrupt anything." Chelsey came around her desk and reached out for a hug.

"Hi, Xavier."

"Argh," he grunted, pecking Chelsey on the forehead, leaving her office.

"I hope he doesn't hate me for interrupting you guys."

"He'll get over it, and the man can't go one day without seeing or touching me." Chelsey plopped down in her chair.

"I understand. Mason's the same way."

"So what brings you by today?"

"I had to make a deposit, so I asked if you were working today."

"Being the manager, I end up working all hours of the day," Chelsey replied, fixing her top.

"Have you been to the club lately?" I asked.

"Xavier took me a week before everything happened, but lately, no."

"I plan on going back."

"You should, as an adult. Owning our pleasure is no one's business," Chelsey ranted.

"I needed to hear that."

"Are you ready for the interview with Lisa?"

"Yes, I plan on telling the truth. Whatever happens after that, who knows."

She extended a hand, gripping my right palm.

"No matter what, you have our support."

"Thanks but let me get out of here. I doubt Xavier has left."

"He gets grumpy from time to time, now that he's running multiple gyms."

"How's that going?"

"Amazing. Everyone wants to invest in his company. I hardly see him because of our schedules."

"As a girl in love, take the time to connect with your man."

"You're right. Maybe I can go to lunch with him now," Chelsey mumbled, checking her watch.

Standing, we hugged once again, and she walked me out of her office. We noticed Xavier talking to the security guard.

"He never left." I chuckled.

"Keep me updated, and I'll talk soon." Chelsey waved good-bye, and I nodded, walking past Xavier.

"She's all yours," I whispered to him.

"I know," Xavier answered, smirking.

CHAPTER 9

SENATOR HILL

A week later.

I sat in the chair at Lisa's news station, preparing to give an interview and discuss where things stood with my career. Some fellow Congressmen tried to get me to resign, but I refused and sent out a statement in the press that I would only do this interview one time and explain how this came to be. Mason still hadn't spoken with his family, but Erica did come out and apologize for getting involved after she tried to defame my name on social media. A grown woman stooped to high school bullying.

"How are you feeling?" Jennifer inquired, standing next to me in the makeup chair.

"Nervous."

"Kyla knows the questions; you should be fine."

"I hope so."

"Just remember to speak from the heart."

A knock at the door interrupted us.

"We're ready for you, Senator Hill," a crew member informed me.

"Okay, thank you," I replied.

48

"Is Mason here yet?" Jennifer asked.

I checked my phone, sliding off the chair. Smoothing my jacket down, I decided to wear a pantsuit for today in my favorite grey color. Something subtle and not over the top to give any critics a chance to overanalyze what I wore. Jennifer and I walked out of the room, heading to the set as I checked my message thread.

"Sorry I'm late." I looked up, hearing Mason speak.

He bent down to give me a hug.

"I thought you weren't coming," I said.

"Traffic," Mason responded, kissing my forehead.

"You'll sit right here, ma'am," the assistant told us.

"Okay. Is Lisa ready?" I questioned, and they looked over at the other crew people.

"Senator Hill, I'm so glad to finally meet you." Barbara Mitchell reached her hand out for a shake.

"Where's Lisa?" I asked.

Barbara was notorious for being a gossip queen and trying to break people down on live TV. I expected Lisa, as my friend, to handle this situation delicately.

"I'm sorry, Lisa's been assigned to another story," Barbara answered, and the director motioned for me to sit down.

"Wait…"

"Action!" the director yelled out.

"Thank you for being with me today. I have Senator Hill joining us," Barbara said.

Barbara turned in her seat, holding up her note cards. I felt my throat close up.

"Senator Hill, please tell me and the audience why you deserve to be in this role?" Barbara questioned.

"Excuse me?"

"Isn't it true you've been frolicking with a married man?"

"That's a lie!"

"According to public opinion, you've been seen at some sex dungeon," Barbara continued, spouting out lies.

"I... I..."

"Please be honest; we as taxpayers want the truth of where our money goes.""

I fiddled with my hands, feeling like I was on the verge of throwing up.

"Barbara, I'm a single woman," I answered.

"But Erica Brownstone says you've been messing with her fiancé?" Barbara held up a notecard.

"I'm not sure where she got that idea, but Mason Norris is single," I scoffed, crossing my legs.

"Well, some people are saying you're with him for money. I mean his father is the speaker of the house," Barbara brought up.

"I have my own money." I ran my hand through my hair, feeling the lights bearing down on me.

"So the story in the *Daily News* of money being added onto the bill you're proposing is fake?"

A light bulb went off in my head at the mention of the bill I helped sponsor. The only person besides Adam Norris was Congressman Jones. They'd stepped into a different level of sabotage by making it seem like I was stealing money and dating a married man. Clearing my throat, I sat up straight, deepening my stare into her eyes.

"Barbara, my record speaks for itself. What I do in my private life is my business."

"Not if that hinders your job like dating the son of the speaker."

"Not a crime. Yes, it's abnormal, possibly, but he's single, and I'm single."

"Shouldn't you try to present a wholesome image and not some sex fiend?" Barbara said.

"Again, my private life is my business."

"What about these images that are circulating of you being tied up?" Barbara pointed at the screen, showing me in lingerie with a blindfold and Mason behind me.

"Something that shouldn't be shown without my permission. I suggest you take this down right now because I'm done with this interview." I ripped off my microphone and stormed offset. I heard her call my name, but I didn't care to listen to a full-on setup trying to embarrass me.

"Let's go," I told Jennifer, grabbing my purse and jacket with Mason next to me.

"Senator Hill! Wait, please," Barbara shouted, stopping me at the door.

"I was only doing my job," Barbara said.

"That was bullshit, and you know it."

"People like you think once you get into politics, it's all cookies and rainbows."

"You're right. I thought another woman would understand what I'm going through."

She shrugged her shoulders.

"If you'd stop slutting yourself out, then…"

I punched her in the face, interrupting her last words.

"Shit," Mason said.

"I think we need to go," Jennifer remarked, pulling me by my arm out of the news station. I pulled my phone out of my pocket, dialing Lisa's number.

* * *

LISA FLEW BACK INTO TOWN, and I called the girls meeting at my house to discuss the events that happened since the interview.

"I promise I didn't know anything about this," Lisa pleaded.

"Who made the change?"

"My producer called and said an important story came in, and they needed me out of town," Lisa replied.

"Sounds like Mason's father probably set you up," Chelsey explained.

"I'm starting to think that as well."

"What can I do?" Kyla said.

"Honestly, nothing."

"Maybe we can do another interview," Lisa mentioned, lifting the wine glass.

"I'm done with interviews."

"What did Mason say about everything?" Kyla queried.

"He's working with his lawyers to get the pictures removed from the internet." I flopped down in my seat, exhausted from having to deal with more drama of the recurring video of me punching Barbara.

"I have to say, you hit Barbara good. She hasn't spoken your name once," Lisa said.

"That's not funny, Lisa."

"You're right, but she deserved that punch." Lisa raised her hands in the air, surrendering.

"Maybe I should just resign."

"No!" everybody answered at the same time.

"Mason will fix this," Jennifer said.

"He's probably thinking of ways he can distance himself from me."

"Are you still staying with him?" Chelsey wondered.

"Yeah, I just came here today because I wanted to meet with you guys."

"Things will blow over; give it time," Lisa stated.

"Turn that up," Jennifer called out, pointing at the TV screen with breaking news.

"We have breaking news coming from the Capitol," Barbara spoke into the camera.

"Isn't that Adam Norris?" Lisa pointed at the screen. I nodded.

"Today, I'd like to show my support for Senator Hill and

state that she's been nothing but a professional at all levels," Adam stated.

My mouth dropped in surprise at the complete change in his tone for me.

"The investigation concluded that Senator Hill did nothing wrong, and her private life is that... private," Adam said, reading from a piece of paper.

"What about the bill, sir?" a reporter called out.

"It's come to my attention that some things were mishandled by my staff. Senator Hill did nothing wrong," Adam replied.

I smirked, knowing Mason probably had something to do with his father throwing his support around me.

"Again, Senator Hill is a fine congresswoman and deserves the support from the rest of her colleagues and me."

Jennifer turned the TV down, raising a glass toward me and passing one to Chelsey and Lisa.

"Time to celebrate! To Senator Hill." Jennifer popped the bottle of red wine open, pouring in each of our glasses. I was ready to sulk away with alcohol all night, but now things were looking up for me.

CHAPTER 10

MASON

Three hours earlier

My father glared at me as I stood in his chambers with an envelope in my hand, ready to bring his entire career down. I tried to always stay out of his way, and he stayed out of mine, but coming for the woman I loved was something I couldn't stand for any longer.

"I'm not going to ask you again." He dropped the envelope on his desk.

"What's this?" He picked it up, turning it around removing the documents.

"Something you'd prefer to not get out."

Adam Norris was stealing not only from his charity but taking bribes from the businesses he approved to get government contracts. I had my private investigator dig into his background who brought me something I could use as a final negotiating tactic. I didn't want to stoop to this level with my own father, but he left me no choice. Congressman Jones co-sponsored some of these bills, and the one Maya proposed would have put a spotlight on what they were doing. So it was easy to make her seem like some homewrecker and have Erica pretend in the media like we were engaged.

"Where did you get this?"

"I have my sources."

"Do you understand what you're doing, Mason?"

"Yeah, protecting my woman."

"This would hurt your mother and our family!" he shouted.

"Then I suggest you do the right thing."

"It wasn't my idea."

"Money was always more important to you."

"You're selfish."

He slammed the papers on his desk, jumping up and pointing in my face.

"I'm your father! She's—"

"Say it! I dare you." I glared at him.

"Get out of my office."

"Gladly, and I suggest you make a statement publicly, or this will go viral."

"Mason, think about this before you make a bigger problem."

"All my life, you've tried to control me, and now it stops."

"We're family!" he argued.

"No, you want me to follow like the rest of your minions and make you look good while robbing people blind." I pointed to the documents on his desk.

"Silly fool."

"Does Mom know?" I questioned.

"No," he muttered, running a hand down his face.

"What happened to you?"

"It's called politics. You have to play with the big boys."

"Sell your soul for money."

He snarled, coming around his desk and pushing his finger in my face.

"Go ahead, judge me, but this lifestyle helped you get to where you are now."

"There you go once again, always trying to act as if I owe you something."

"Get out of my office." He pointed toward the door.

"Just remember, I have copies of everything."

* * *

THE NEXT DAY, finally making it home, I was exhausted after working overtime to make sure Maya didn't have any more issues with my father and his team. I had planned on going to the club to finish paperwork after closing the deal to open more clubs in Chicago and New York. My stomach growled as I locked my door and headed into the kitchen to grab a bottle of water. I gulped it down, standing at the counter, letting tiredness peak. Feeling my phone vibrate, I groaned, not wanting to talk to anyone. I pulled it out and opened the messages, seeing Maya's name pop up.

MyWorld: Come upstairs.

I was intrigued by her being here since we rarely stayed at my place or the club. I finished off the bottle and tossed it in the trash. Turning the phone on Do Not Disturb, I jogged upstairs and pushed the bedroom door open, smirking at the display before me.

"This is a surprise." Maya was completely naked, lying in my bed with only her red heels on.

"I hoped for a good surprise." She crawled off the bed, stalking over to me with determination in her eyes. Grasping my hand, she walked me over to the bed and pushed me down.

"What do I owe for this surprise?"

Maya stood in front of me with her hands on both sides of my face, bent down to peck my lips.

"Thank you for supporting me with your family."

"I'd do anything for you," I assured, running a hand up her thigh.

"I believe you, Mason."

"So does this mean…" I helped her to straddle my lap. Clasping my hand behind her neck, I pulled her in close, forcing my tongue inside and exploring her fully. Rubbing against her engorged clit, I snarled, wanting to eat her pussy and listening to her cry out in pleasure. Tossing her on the bed, I removed my shirt and pants, and stared into her eyes. Tweaking her brown nipple, I squeezed, taking my favorite pillows into my mouth at the same time.

"Mason… Oh God—"

"Let me hear you, baby."

Feeling her leaking down her thighs, I watched her fall back into the pillows in a daze. Wanting to tease her some more, I pinched her nipple, hearing her moans get louder.

"Baby, you're so wet," I murmured, watching her juices cover my fingers.

She shuddered against me, dipping one, two, then three fingers into her folds.

"I'm going to fuck the shit out of you." My breath brushed against her ear.

"Yesss!" she panted, opening her legs wider. Sucking on her neck, I slid my dick in and paused, feeling her tight, warm core surrounding me. I bent down, sucking one plump breast in my mouth, watching her squirm in my arms as I slowly moved in and out.

"Uhhhh… fuck." She dug her nails in my back.

"I'm drowning here, baby; you feel so good."

Kissing on her lips, our eyes locked, and my chest swelled with love knowing she was the one for me. Squeezing her thighs, I pulled back, thrusting faster as I felt her getting close to her climax.

"Come for me, Maya," I demanded.

Gripping the sheets, there was a look of rawness, longing for this to never end, and I'd make it my mission to always give her body pleasure.

"Oh my God! I'm coming," she screamed, running a hand down my chest, brushing against my balls.

"Aghhh, shit!" I released, falling over on the bed beside her, out of breath.

She leaned over, running her tongue over my nipple. I grasped the back of her head, cupping her sex.

"Mmmmm…" She opened her legs wider.

Wrapping a hand around her throat, I said, "Next time I have to use the flogger with you." I smacked her ass.

"Promise?"

I grinned. "Keep teasing me like this…" Rubbing her back, I crawled between her legs. "How are you feeling about things?"

"Did you talk to your father?"

"You don't need to worry about that."

Maya smiled, caressing my cheek.

"I'm hungry."

"What are you hungry for?" Gliding my tongue down her stomach, I noticed her breathing heightened as her eyes rolled in the back of her head.

"What would you suggest?"

"Maybe I could cook your favorite lasagna with red wine and Italian bread."

She sucked in her breath when I slid a finger across her bud.

"That sounds good." Maya reached down, placing her hands on my shoulders.

"Perfect."

I placed another kiss on her lips, moving off her and reaching for my robe. Maya wrapped the cover around her naked body.

"When are we going back to Club Seek?" She placed her arm up on the bed, cupping the side of her face.

"I didn't think you'd want to go back so soon." Pulling her robe off the back of the door, I helped her out of bed to follow me to the kitchen.

Maya stepped in front of me, cupping my face and staring into my eyes.

"What we do isn't wrong, and I won't let anyone dictate our relationship." She bit my bottom lip, moaning and sucking on my lips, snaking her tongue around mine. Wrapping my arms around her waist, I groaned, wanting to go for another round but hearing my stomach growl at the same time.

"More of that later. I'm starving." I pulled back from the kiss.

"Yes, sir. I love you," she said.

"I love you more."

SENATOR HILL

Two Years Later.

I turned the TV off from the endless cycle of reporters talking about my life choices, and what I'd done in the past and how my life with Mason started in not the most realistic of ways. People didn't know me but claimed to speak with sources that could verify every little detail of when I first lost my tooth as a baby. Chuckling at the thought, I finished typing out emails and sending text messages. I rose from my seat, walking out of my office after finishing another meeting with Jennifer. Today's debate was about funding for our schools. I forced the speaker to finally listen to what I had to say after he found out Mason and I eloped. I wasn't trying to hide what we had and how we started, but I wanted to keep my personal life private. After the storm that almost brought me down, my goal was to be attuned with the people I knew and aware that it may seem friendly, but the beast of politics was very much real.

"You ready to go to lunch?" I turned around at the voice that kept me weak in the knees every night in our bedroom. He still had that devilish smile and sexy full lips that I missed kissing when I got out of bed this morning.

"I didn't expect you for another ten minutes," I spoke, standing from my desk, and headed into his open arms.

He kissed me on the cheek, lifted my chin, and bit my bottom lip. He slid a hand around my waist to pull me in close.

"Daddy!" our daughter called out, trying to push my face away. I chuckled at her movements. She was so spoiled and only wanted to be the number one girl in his eyes. Malia reminded me of Mason's cocky demeanor in the early days of our courtship. He was determined to make me fall in love, and I tried to push him away, but love broke through the walls, and I more than made up for our time, learning to balance my career and family life. Mason held my hand while holding Malia in his arms, escorting us over to the conference room. I was making an announcement on the launch of a new program for women in business after negotiating enough votes for a year to pass the bill.

"You two look so cute together." Jennifer walked up next to me, carrying my notes.

I smiled. "Thanks. Is everybody here?"

Tony stood in his usual spot, holding the door open for us, and the reality of winning re-election for another term was the most important thing to me. I was grateful for all the support. Since the events of the past still ran through social media, I had to be careful with how I responded at times.

"Senator Hill, are you planning to run again?" a reporter in the back yelled out. The room went completely quiet, and the stares focused on me. Today's announcement was about the outstanding accomplishments we'd made, but it seemed gossip and drama might cloud the subject. I glanced at Mason and Malia. He kissed her on the cheek, winked at me, and I smiled, knowing he supported me in my decision.

"I was waiting to do this at another time. But I can announce that—"

"OMG!" Another reporter from CBG News shoved their phone to the reporter next to them.

I cleared my throat, about to respond.

"Is that Lisa Reyes?" Hearing Lisa's name caused me to tense. I covered the microphone with my hand, stepping over to Jennifer.

"You need to call Lisa," Jennifer whispered, passing me her phone. I saw a broadcast video of the news station where she worked with a breaking news story with Lisa and Morris in a video clip at Club Seek.

"This can't be happening," I mumbled under my breath.

"Senator Hill, what do you have to say about the video?"

"Senator Hill, do you think Lisa did this on purpose?"

Everyone threw questions at me, and all I wanted to do was call Lisa and see how she was doing.

"Lisa Reyes is a close friend, and I ask that everyone respect her privacy." Mason reached for my hand as we walked out of the room together. Keeping my head high, I shook inside, feeling sick to my stomach that someone was doing the same thing to Lisa they did to me.

"Senator Hill! Senator Hill!" Photographers continued shouting my name for attention, heading toward our town car. Tony opened the door, and I slid inside, with Mason next to me. I unbuttoned my jacket, reaching into my pocket to grab my cell. Pulling up the video again showed her in a red lingerie set. Morris was behind her, gripping her hair in his hands. Closing the video, I went to social media, and there was non-stop coverage of the video being replayed and calls for her to step down.

"I can't believe this is happening."

"Mommy, what's wrong?" Malia asked, laying her head on my shoulder. I lifted her in my arms and placed her in my lap.

"Just remember, no matter what happens in life, Malia, seek out what makes you happy."

Tony clicked on the turn signal to pull into traffic, Jennifer turned her phone off from the constant alerts, and Mason grasped my hand and brought it up to his lips.

"Are you having regrets?" Mason wondered.

"I only regret never putting this first." I motioned my hand between the three of us, and a smile tugged at the corner of his lips.

* * *

I HOPE you enjoyed Maya and Mason's story. Please also check out "**Seeking To Touch Book 2**" here https://books2read. com/u/47N7xR

If you love brother's best friend romance then you'll love "**Sensual**" **here** https://books2read.com/u/49lYYM with a host of characters intertwined.

Check out Bodyguard Romance here *"Protecting Bria"* https://books2read.com/u/bQJkjd

Please also check out my *"Haven"* https://books2read.- com/u/4jAvyZ a steamy enemies to lovers romance.

Have you checked out "**His Peace Her Pleasure**" click here https://books2read.com/u/3JJr0P a billionaire, steamy romance.

Lisa, a TV news anchor, is used to pressure at the job, but when she learns that someone is about to leak a video of her at a sex club, the pressure could make her life implode. If she doesn't do something to stop it, she'll lose her job, her family will disown her, and that's only the beginning.

Enlisting the help of her best friend's husband's business partner and security agent to help her may be her only hope. If they can find out who is behind the scheme, her worries are over… she hopes.

Can they figure out who is out to ruin her before it's too late?

ORDER OF SERIES

Seek To Please Book 1
Seek To Touch Book 2
Seek To Bare Book 3
Seek To Love Book 4

1. What's the name of the club?
   2. What's the name of Mason's business partner?
   3. Did Mason forgive his father too easily?
   4. What's the name of Maya and Mason's daughter?
   5. What's the name of the reporter that interviewed Maya?
   6. Who worked with Mason's father to destroy Maya?

By Keke Renée:
  Wet Heat
  His Peace, Her Pleasure
  Baby, It's Cold Outside
  Love Don't Live Here Anymore, Book 1
  Love Don't Live Here Anymore, Book 2
  Every Time We Touch (A Wet Heat Novelette)
  Sensual
  Taste
  Haven
  Protecting Bria
  One Night Only-A Novelette Book 1
  Cassian and Savannah-Love By Design Book 2
  Deidra's Love-Love By Design Book 3

"Starting small can lead to bigger things."
    -KeKe Renée

ABOUT THE AUTHOR

A Tennessee native, and California dreaming Author KeKe Renée is living and striving to continue her passion of writing Short Story romances from Erotic, Paranormal, and Urban Fiction.

Want to know what happens next?

Follow me on website to find out the latest about the next release.

Reviews are the lifeblood of the publishing world. They're read, appreciated, and needed. Please consider taking the time to leave a few words on Goodreads, or Bookbub.

Sign up for updates and sneak peeks at the site below.

https://landing.mailerlite.com/webforms/landing/r7j2s6

The home of authors African American, Interracial, Women's Fiction, Fantasy, Erotic, and Contemporary Romance novels. Along with Thriller, Suspense, Poetry, Beauty, and Style Books. Thank you for taking the time out to visit. Join our mailing list to stay updated with new releases and blog posts.